NORM

For Lin, Yong and Andy

NORM

SYLVIA LIANG

Thames & Hudson

Hi! I'm Normal. Everyone calls me Norm.
I look exactly the way a normal person looks.

These are my friends, Plain and Simple.

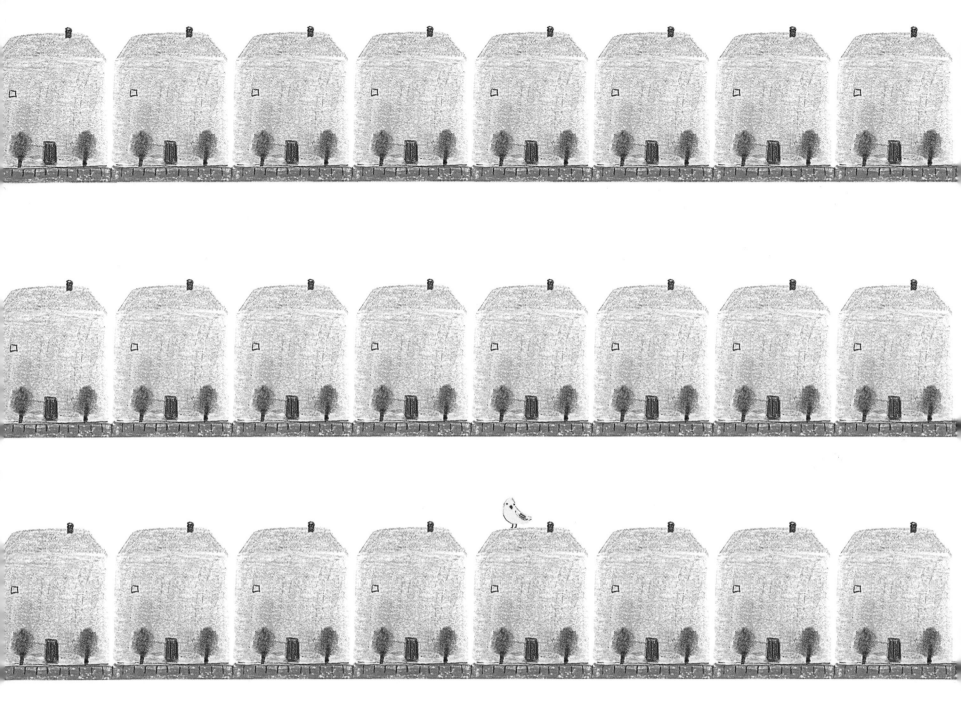

This is our village. As you can see, it is very tidy and orderly.

That's because everyone in my village has a ruler.
We spend all day measuring things!

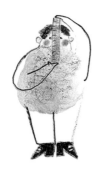

We measure ourselves,

and everything around us.

If something isn't the right size,
we find somewhere to hide it.

If someone stands out, we
politely look the other way.

Things are pretty perfect the way they are.

We know the shape of every tree.

And the size of every flower
(28 cm if you need to know).

At 3 o'clock every afternoon,
Plain and Simple and I drink tea.

Our trees are matching. So are our cups.
Plain tells us one of his terrible jokes.
Simple and I sometimes laugh.

At 3.30 pm, we trim our trees.
But it turns out that today is not a day
for tree trimming.

Not when a strange yellow bird
makes an appearance.

And not when it won't sit
still long enough to be
measured.

And certainly not after it leads me to an extraordinarily big flower. It's unlike any flower I have ever seen before.

This flower is the size of a house.
It is much bigger than my ruler.

I look around for something I can measure.

'At least this ladybird is a normal size.'

But then a rustle in the bushes brings
an even more unexpected spectacle!

It's a girl. She is unlike
any girl I have met before.

Her name is Odette. I call her Odd for short. Odd is very friendly.

But her neighbourhood is strange.

I approach with caution, as any
normal person would.

In this town, houses are made
of boots, and boots are green.
'Oh,' I groan, 'Whatever next?!'

Odd introduces me to a throng
of different friendly faces.

There is Eddie. He makes sweets
called Clouded Apples.

The recipe?

'Equal measures of apple, sugar
and imagination,' he tells me
with a wink.

Lady Lily is a milliner.
She decorates her hats with
sea creatures.

Mr King tells me about musical maths.
He counts out the beat with his feet.

Professor John is
hopelessly messy,
but the stories he
tells make the world
melt away.

As for me? I show them
what I do best.

But Odd has one more thing to share with me.

'Norm,' she sighs, 'if you
focus on your ruler all
the time...'

'... you'll miss the things that
will amaze you in this world.'

Sure enough, when I stop measuring...

... I discover the most curious surprises.

I think about my friends back home.
Plain's terrible jokes, Simple's funny laugh.
It occurs to me that neither of them
is very normal either.

It's the things that can't be measured that I like the most about them.

Odd and her friends invite
me to visit anytime I want.

Back home, Plain and Simple
are pleased to see me.

I even think they like my new dance moves.

When we sit down for 3 o'clock tea,
Plain tells us a joke.

'That's not a joke!' I cry. 'Jokes are
supposed to be funny!'

We laugh so hard, we
almost spill our tea.

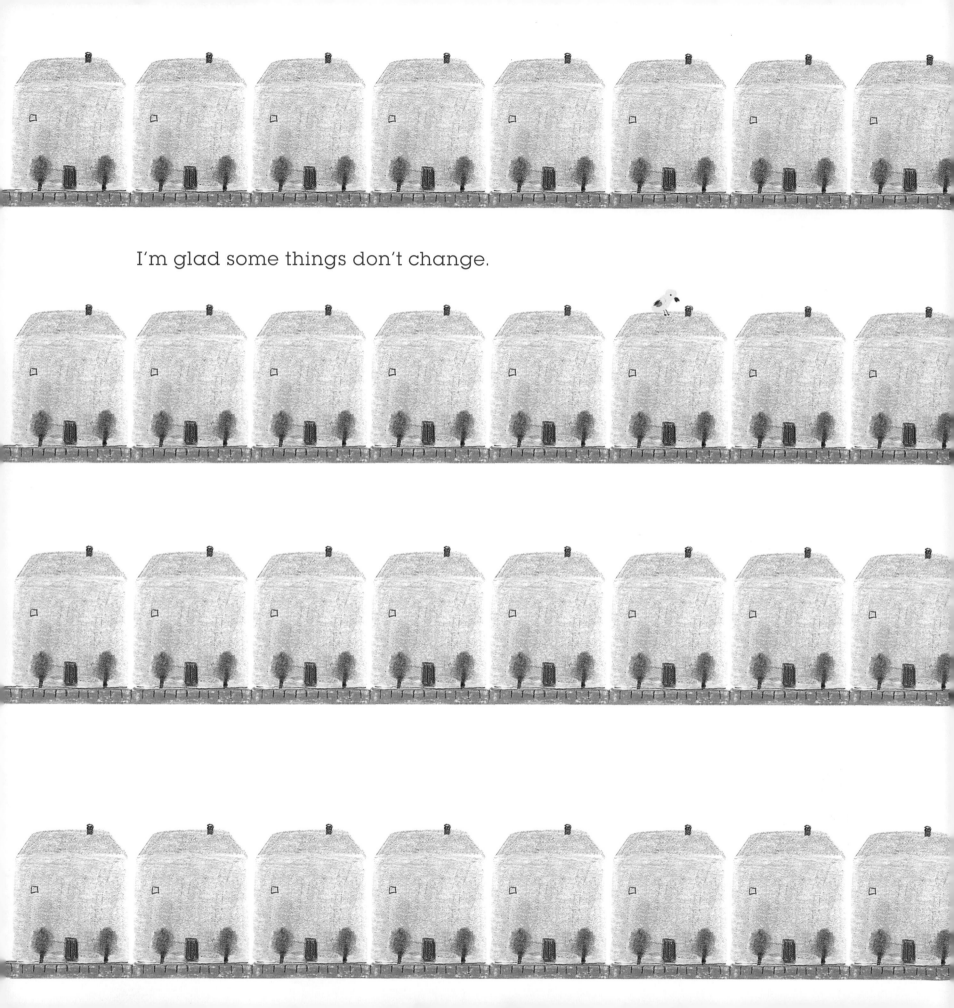

I'm glad some things don't change.

But there's always room for something new...

First published in the United Kingdom in 2019 by Thames & Hudson Ltd,
181A High Holborn, London WC1V 7QX

Norm © 2019 Sylvia Liang (Yuchen Liang)

British Library Cataloguing-in-Publication Data
A catalogue record for this book is available from the British Library

ISBN 978-0-500-65161-2

Printed and bound in China by Toppan Leefung Printing Limited

To find out about all our publications, please visit **www.thamesandhudson.com**.
There you can subscribe to our e-newsletter, browse or download our current catalogue,
and buy any titles that are in print.